For two great sisters, Emily and Alice . . .
"To there!" —L. N.

For Jessica and Ben —L. M.

Text © 2011 by Laura Numeroff.
Illustrations © 2011 by Lynn Munsinger.

Library of Congress Cataloging-in-Publication Data available.
ISBN 978-0-8118-6601-9

Book design by Eloise Leigh and Aimee Gauthier.
Typeset in Eureka.
The illustrations in this book were rendered in
watercolors, pen and ink, and pencil.

Manufactured by Toppan Leefung, Da Ling Shan Town,
Dongguan, China, in May 2011.

1 3 5 7 9 10 8 6 4 2

This product conforms to CPSIA 2008.

Chronicle Books LLC
680 Second Street, San Francisco, California 94107

www.chroniclekids.com

What PUPPIES Do Best

By Laura Numeroff 🐾 Illustrated by Lynn Munsinger

chronicle books·san francisco

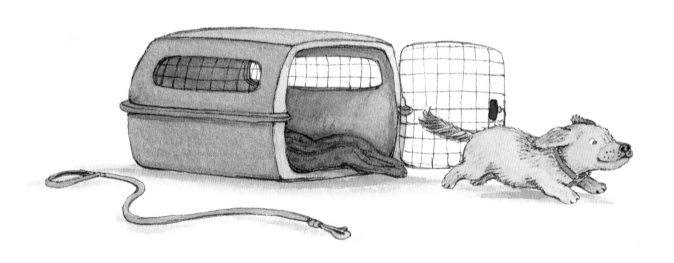

Puppies can wake you up
in the morning,

try to climb onto your bed,

and give you a kiss.

Puppies can chase a ball,

learn how to sit,

and give you their paw.

Puppies can dig holes
in the yard,

track mud into the house,

and make a big mess.

Puppies can greet you
when you get home,

run around in circles,

and roll over for a belly rub.

Puppies can go on walks,

make friends with other puppies,

and run alongside you!

Puppies can play tug-of-war,

take a bath,

and get you all wet.

Puppies can snuggle with you,

get cozy in their bed,

and give you a kiss good night!

But best of all . . .

puppies can give
you lots and lots
of love.